The Bedtime Story-Books

The Adventures of Prickly Porky

By THORNTON W. BURGESS

Illustrated by HARRISON CADY

PUBLISHERS

Grosset & Dunlap

NEW YORK

Contents

[v]

CONTENTS

[vi]

Illustrations

[*vii*]

ILLUSTRATIONS

I

Happy Jack Squirrel Makes a Find

HAPPY JACK SQUIRREL had had a wonderful day. He had found some big chestnut trees that he had never seen before, and which promised to give him all the nuts he would want for all the next winter. Now he was thinking of going home, for it was getting late in the after- noon. He looked out across the open field where Mr. Goshawk had nearly caught him that morning. His home was on the other side.

"It's a long way 'round," said Happy Jack to himself, "but it is best to be safe and sure."

So Happy Jack started on his long journey around the open field. Now Happy Jack's eyes are bright, and there is very little that Happy Jack does not see. So, as he was jumping from one tree to another, he spied something down on the ground which excited his curiosity.

"I must stop and see what that

[12]

is," said Happy Jack. So down the tree he ran, and in a few minutes he had found the queer thing which had caught his eyes. It was smooth and black and white, and at one end it was very sharp with a tiny little barb. Happy Jack found it out by pricking himself with it.

"Ooch," he cried, and dropped the queer thing. Pretty soon he noticed there were a lot more on the ground.

"I wonder what they are," said Happy Jack. "They don't grow, for they haven't any roots. They are not thorns, for there is no

[*13*]

plant from which they could come. They are not alive, so what can they be?"

Now Happy Jack's eyes are bright, but sometimes he doesn't use them to the very best advantage. He was so busy examining the queer things on the ground that he never once thought to look up in the tops of the trees. If he had, perhaps he would not have been so much puzzled. As it was he just gathered up three or four of the queer things and started on again. On the way he met Peter Rabbit and showed Peter what he had. Now you know

Peter Rabbit is very curious. He just couldn't sit still, but must scamper over to the place Happy Jack Squirrel told him about.

"You'd better be careful, Peter Rabbit; they're very sharp," shouted Happy Jack.

But as usual, Peter was in too much of a hurry to heed what was said to him. Lipperty-lipperty-lip, lipperty-lipperty-lip, went Peter Rabbit through the woods, as fast as his long legs would take him. Then suddenly he squealed and sat down to nurse one of his feet. But he was up again in a flash with an-

[*15*]

other squeal louder than before. Peter Rabbit had found the queer things that Happy Jack Squirrel had told him about. One was sticking in his foot, and one was in the white patch on the seat of his trousers.

II

The Stranger from the North

THE Merry Little Breezes of Old Mother West Wind were excited. Yes, Sir, they certainly were excited. They had met Happy Jack Squirrel and Peter Rabbit, and they were full of the news of the queer things that Happy Jack and Peter Rabbit had found over in the Green Forest. They hurried this way and that way over the Green Meadows and told everyone they met. Finally they reached the Smiling Pool and excitedly told Grandfather Frog all about it.

Grandfather Frog smoothed down his white-and-yellow waist-coat and looked very wise, for you know that Grandfather Frog is very old.

"Pooh," said Grandfather Frog. "I know what they are."

"What?" cried all the Merry Little Breezes together. "Happy Jack says he is sure they do not grow, for there are no strange plants over there."

[18]

HARRISON CADY

*Grandfather Frog smoothed down his white-
and-yellow waistcoat and looked very wise*

Grandfather Frog opened his big mouth and snapped up a foolish green fly that one of the Merry Little Breezes blew over to him.

"Chug-a-rum," said Grandfather Frog. "Things do not have to be on plants in order to grow. Now I am sure that those things grew, and that they did not grow on a plant."

The Merry Little Breezes looked puzzled. "What is there that grows and doesn't grow on a plant?" asked one of them.

"How about the claws on Peter Rabbit's toes and the hair of

[20]

Happy Jack's tail?" asked Grandfather Frog.

The Merry Little Breezes looked foolish. "Of course," they cried. "We didn't think of that. But we are quite sure that these queer things that prick so are not claws, and certainly they are not hair."

"Don't you be too sure," said Grandfather Frog. "You go over to the Green Forest and look up in the treetops instead of down on the ground; then come back and tell me what you find."

Away raced the Merry Little Breezes to the Green Forest and

began to search among the tree-tops. Presently, way up in the top of a big poplar, they found a stranger. He was bigger than any of the little meadow people, and he had long sharp teeth with which he was stripping the bark from the tree. The hair of his coat was long, and out of it peeped a thousand little spears just like the queer things that Happy Jack and Peter Rabbit had told them about.

"Good morning," said the Merry Little Breezes politely.

"Mornin'," grunted the stranger in the treetop.

[22]

"May we ask where you come from?" said one of the Merry Little Breezes politely.

"I come from the North Woods," said the stranger and then went on about his business, which seemed to be to strip every bit of the bark from the tree and eat it.

III

Prickly Porky Makes Friends

THE Merry Little Breezes soon
spread the news over the
Green Meadows and through the
Green Forest that a stranger had
come from the North. At once
all the little meadow people and
forest folk made some excuse to
go over to the big poplar tree
where the stranger was so busy
eating. At first he was very shy

[*24*]

and had nothing to say. He was a queer fellow, and he was so big, and his teeth were so sharp and so long, that his visitors kept their distance.

Reddy Fox, who you know is a great boaster and likes to brag of how smart he is and how brave he is, came with the rest of the little meadow people.

"Pooh," exclaimed Reddy Fox. "Who's afraid of that fellow?"

Just then the stranger began to come down the tree. Reddy backed away.

"It looks as if you were afraid, Reddy Fox," said Peter Rabbit.

[25]

"I'm not afraid of anything," said Reddy Fox, and swelled himself up to look twice as big as he really is.

"It seems to me I hear Bowser the Hound," piped up Striped Chipmunk.

Now Striped Chipmunk had not heard Bowser the Hound at all when he spoke, but just then there was the patter of heavy feet among the dried leaves, and sure enough, there was Bowser himself. My, how everybody did run— everybody but the stranger from the North. He kept on coming down the tree just the same.

HARRISON CADY

*My, how everybody did run—everybody but
the stranger from the North*

Bowser saw him and stopped in surprise. He had never seen anything quite like this big, dark fellow.

"Bow, wow, wow!" shouted Bowser in his deepest voice.

Now when Bowser used that great deep voice of his, he was accustomed to seeing all the little meadow people and forest folk run, but this stranger did not even hurry. Bowser was so surprised that he just stood still and stared. Then he growled his deepest growl. Still the stranger paid no attention to him. Bowser did not know what to make of it.

[28]

"I'll teach that fellow a lesson," said Bowser to himself. "I'll shake him and shake him and shake him until he hasn't any breath left."

By this time the stranger was down on the ground and starting for another tree, minding his own business. Then something happened. Bowser made a rush at him, and instead of running, what do you suppose the stranger did? He just rolled himself up in a tight ball with his head tucked down in his waistcoat. When he was rolled up that way, all the little spears hidden in the hair of

[29]

his coat stood right out until he looked like a great chestnut bur. Bowser stopped short. Then he reached out his nose and sniffed at this queer thing. Slap! The tail of the stranger struck Bowser the Hound right across the side of his face, and a dozen of those little spears were left sticking there just like pins in a pin-cushion.

"Wow! wow! wow! wow!" yelled Bowser at the top of his lungs, and started for home with his tail between his legs, and yelling with every jump. Then the stranger unrolled himself and

[*30*]

smiled, and all the little meadow people and forest folk who had been watching shouted aloud for joy.

And this is the way that Prickly Porky the Porcupine made friends.

IV

Peter Rabbit Has Some Startling News

LITTLE Mrs. Peter Rabbit, who used to be Little Miss Fuzzytail, sat at the edge of the dear Old Briar-patch, anxiously looking over toward the Green Forest. She was worried. There was no doubt about it. Little Mrs. Peter was very much worried. Why didn't Peter come home? She did wish that he would be content to stay close by the dear Old Briar-patch. For her part, she couldn't see why under the sun he wanted to go way over to the Green Forest. He was always having dreadful adventures and narrow escapes over there, and yet, in spite of all she could say, he would persist in going there. She didn't feel easy in her mind one minute while he was out of her sight. To be sure, he always turned up all right, but she couldn't help feeling that sometime his dreadful curiosity would get him into trouble that he couldn't get out of, and so

[*33*]

every time he went to the Green Forest, she was sure, absolutely sure, that she would never see him again.

Peter used to laugh at her and tell her that she was a foolish little dear, and that he was perfectly able to take care of himself. Then, when he saw how worried she was, he would promise to be very, very careful and never do anything rash or foolish. But he wouldn't promise not to go to the Green Forest. No, Sir, Peter wouldn't promise that. You see, he has so many friends over

[*34*]

there, and there is always so much news to be gathered that he just couldn't keep away. Once or twice he had induced Mrs. Peter to go with him, but she had been frightened almost out of her skin every minute, for it seemed to her that there was danger lurking behind every tree and under every bush. It was all very well for Chatterer the Red Squirrel and Happy Jack the Gray Squirrel, who could jump from tree to tree, but she didn't think it a safe and proper place for a sensible Rabbit, and she said so.

This particular morning she was unusually anxious. Peter had been gone all night. Usually he was home by the time Old Mother West Wind came down from the Purple Hills and emptied her children, the Merry Little Breezes, out of her big bag to play all day on the Green Meadows, but this morning Old Mother West Wind had been a long time gone about her business, and still there was no sign of Peter.

"Something has happened. I just know something has happened!" she wailed.

[*36*]

"Oh, Peter, Peter, Peter Rabbit,
  Why will you be so heedless?
  Why will you take such dreadful risks,
  So foolish and so needless?"

"Don't worry. Peter is smart enough to take care of himself," cried one of the Merry Little Breezes, who happened along just in time to overhear her. "He'll be home pretty soon. In fact, I think I see him coming now."

Mrs. Peter looked in the direction that the Merry Little Breeze was looking, and sure enough, there was Peter. He was heading straight for the dear Old Briar-patch, and he was running as if he were trying to show how fast he could run. Mrs. Peter's heart gave a frightened thump. "It must be that Reddy or Granny Fox or Old Man Coyote is right at his heels," thought she, but look as hard as she would, she could see nothing to make Peter run so.

In a few minutes he reached her side. His eyes were very wide, and it was plain to see that he was bursting with important news.

"What is it, Peter? Do tell me quick! Have you had another nar-

[38]

row escape?" gasped little Mrs. Peter.

Peter nodded while he panted for breath. "There's another stranger in the Green Forest, a terrible-looking fellow without legs or head or tail, and he almost caught me!" panted Peter.

[39]

V

Peter Rabbit Tells His Story

WHEN Peter Rabbit could get his breath after his long, hard run from the Green Forest to the dear Old Briar-patch, he had a wonderful story to tell. It was all about a stranger in the Green Forest, and to have heard Peter tell about it, you would have thought, as Mrs. Peter did, that it was a very terrible stranger, for it had no legs, and it had no head, and it had no tail. At least, that is what Peter said.

"You see, it was this way," declared Peter. "I had stopped longer than I meant to in the Green Forest, for you know, my dear, I always try to be home by the time jolly, round, red Mr. Sun gets out of bed and Old Mother West Wind gets down on the Green Meadows." Mrs. Peter nodded. "But somehow time slipped away faster than I thought for, or else Mr. Sun got up earlier than usual," continued

Peter. Then he stopped. That last idea was a new one and it struck Peter as a good one. "I do believe that that is just what happened—Mr. Sun must have made a mistake and crawled out of bed earlier than usual," he cried.

Mrs. Peter looked as if she very much doubted it, but she didn't say anything, and so Peter went on with his story.

"I had just realized how light it was and had started for home, hurrying with all my might, when I heard a little noise at the top of the hill where Prickly Porky the Porcupine lives. Of course, I

thought it was Prickly himself
starting out for his breakfast, and
I looked up with my mouth open
to say hello. But I didn't say
hello. No, Sir, I didn't say a
word. I was too scared. There,
just starting down the hill
straight toward me, was the most
dreadful creature that ever has
been seen in the Green Forest!
It didn't have any legs, and it
didn't have any head, and it
didn't have any tail, and it was
coming straight after me so fast
that I had all I could do to get
out of the way!" Peter's eyes grew
very round and wide as he said

[43]

this. "I took one good look, and then I jumped. My gracious, how I did jump!" he continued. "Then I started for home just as fast as ever I could make my legs go, and here I am, and mighty glad to be here!"

Mrs. Peter had listened with her mouth wide open. When Peter finished, she closed it with a snap and hopped over and felt of his head.

"Are you sick, Peter?" she asked anxiously.

Peter stared at her. "Sick! Me sick! Not a bit of it!" he exclaimed. "Never felt better in my

*Mrs. Peter had listened with her mouth
wide open*

life, save that I am a little tired from my long run. What a silly question! Do I look sick?"

"No-o," replied little Mrs. Peter slowly. "No-o, you don't look sick, but you talk as if there were something the matter with your head. I think you must be just a little lightheaded, Peter, or else you have taken a nap somewhere and had a bad dream. Did I understand you to say that this dreadful creature has no legs, and yet that it chased you?"

"That's what I said!" snapped Peter a wee bit crossly, for he saw

[46]

that Mrs. Peter didn't believe a word of his story.

"Will you please tell me how any creature in the Green Forest or out of it, for that matter, can possibly chase anyone unless it has legs or wings, and you didn't say anything about its having wings," demanded Mrs. Peter.

Peter scratched his head in great perplexity. Suddenly he had a happy thought. "Mr. Blacksnake runs fast enough, but he doesn't have legs, does he?" he asked in triumph.

Little Mrs. Peter looked a bit

[47]

discomfited. "No-o," she admitted slowly, "he doesn't have legs; but I never could understand how he runs without them."

"Well, then," snapped Peter, "if he can run without legs, why can't other creatures? Besides, this one didn't run exactly; it rolled. Now I've told you all I'm going to. I need a long nap, after all I've been through, so don't let anyone disturb me."

"I won't," replied Mrs. Peter meekly. "But, Peter, if I were you, I wouldn't tell that story to anyone else."

[48]

VI

Peter Has To Tell His Story Many Times

Once you start a story you cannot call
*   it back;*
It travels on and on and on and ever
*   on, alack!*

THAT is the reason why you should always be sure that a story you repeat is a good story. Then you will be glad to have it travel on and on and on, and will never want to call it back. But if you tell a story that isn't true or nice, the time is almost sure to come when you will want to call it back and cannot. You see, stories are just like rivers—they run on and on forever. Little Mrs. Peter Rabbit knew this, and that is why she advised Peter not to tell anyone else the strange story he had told her of the dreadful creature without legs or head or tail that had chased him in the Green Forest. Peter knew by that that she didn't believe a word of it, but he was too tired and sleepy to argue with her then, so he settled himself comfortably for a nice long nap.

When Peter awoke, the first thing he thought of was the

[*50*]

terrible creature he had seen in
the Green Forest. The more he
thought about it, the more impossible it seemed, and he didn't
wonder that Mrs. Peter had advised him not to repeat it.

"I won't," said Peter to himself. "I won't repeat it to a soul.
No one will believe it. The truth
is, I can hardly believe it myself.
I'll just keep my tongue still."

But unfortunately for Peter,
one of the Merry Little Breezes
of Old Mother West Wind had
heard Peter tell the story to Mrs.
Peter, and it was such a wonderful and curious and unbelievable
story that the Merry Little Breeze

[51]

straightway repeated it to everybody he met, and soon Peter Rabbit began to receive callers who wanted to hear the story all over again from Peter himself. So Peter was obliged to repeat it ever so many times, and every time it sounded to him more foolish than before. He had to tell it to Jimmy Skunk and to Johnny Chuck and to Danny Meadow Mouse and to Digger the Badger and to Sammy Jay and to Blacky the Crow and to Striped Chipmunk and to Happy Jack Squirrel and to Bobby Coon and to Unc' Billy Possum and to Old Mr. Toad.

Now, strange to say, no one laughed at Peter, queer as the story sounded. You see, they all remembered how they had laughed at him and made fun of him when he told about the great footprints he had found deep in the Green Forest, and how later it had been proven that he really did see them, for they were made by Buster Bear who had come down from the Great Woods to live in the Green Forest. Then it had been Peter's turn to laugh at them. So now, impossible as this new story sounded, they didn't dare laugh at it.

"I never heard of such a crea-

[53]

ADVENTURES OF PRICKLY PORKY

ture," said Jimmy Skunk, "and I can't quite believe that there is such a one, but it is very clear to me that Peter has seen something strange. You know the old saying that he laughs best who laughs last, and I'm not going to give Peter another chance to have the last laugh and say, 'I told you so.'"

"That is very true," replied Old Mr. Toad solemnly. "Probably Peter has seen something out of the ordinary, and in his excitement he has exaggerated it. The thing to do is to make sure whether or not there is a stranger in the Green Forest. Peter says that it came down the hill where Prickly Porky the Porcupine lives. Someone ought to go ask him what he knows about it. If there is such a terrible creature up there, he ought to have seen it. Why don't you go up there and ask him, Jimmy Skunk? You're not afraid of anybody or anything."

"I will," replied Jimmy promptly, and off he started. You see, he felt very much flattered by Old Mr. Toad's remark, and he couldn't very well refuse, for that would look as if he were afraid, after all.

[55]

VII

Jimmy Skunk Calls on Prickly Porky

A PLAGUE upon Old Mr. Toad!"
grumbled Jimmy, as he am-
bled up the Lone Little Path
through the Green Forest on
his way to the hill where Prickly
Porky lives. "Of course, I'm
not afraid, but just the same I
don't like meddling with things
I don't know anything about. I'm
not afraid of anybody I know of,

[*56*]

HARRISON CADY

"A plague upon Old Mr. Toad!"
grumbled Jimmy

because everybody has the greatest respect for me, but it might
be different with a creature without legs or head or tail. Whoever
heard of such a thing? It gives
me a queer feeling inside."

However, he kept right on, and
as he reached the foot of the hill
where Prickly Porky lives, he
looked sharply in every direction
and listened with all his might
for strange sounds. But there was
nothing unusual to be seen. The
Green Forest looked just as it always did. It was very still and
quiet there save for the cheerful
voice of Redeye the Vireo telling

over and over how happy he was.

"That doesn't sound as if there were any terrible stranger around here," muttered Jimmy.

Then he heard a queer, grunting sound, a very queer sound, that seemed to come from somewhere on the top of the hill. Jimmy grinned as he listened. "That's Prickly Porky telling himself how good his dinner tastes," laughed Jimmy. "Funny how some people do like to hear their own voices."

The contented sound of Prickly Porky's voice made Jimmy feel very sure that there could be

[59]

nothing very terrible about just then, anyway, and so he slowly ambled up the hill, for you know he never hurries. It was an easy matter to find the tree in which Prickly Porky was at work stripping off bark and eating it, because he made so much noise.

"Hello!" said Jimmy Skunk.

Prickly Porky took no notice. He was so busy eating, and making so much noise about it, that he didn't hear Jimmy at all.

"Hello!" shouted Jimmy a little louder. "Hello, there! Are you deaf?" Of course, this wasn't polite at all, but Jimmy was feeling

[*60*]

a little out of sorts because he had had to make this call. This time Prickly Porky looked down.

"Hello yourself, and see how you like it, Jimmy Skunk!" he cried. "Come on up and have some of this nice bark with me." Then Prickly Porky laughed at his own joke, for he knew perfectly well that Jimmy couldn't climb, and that he wouldn't eat bark if he could.

Jimmy made a face at him. "Thank you, I've just dined. Come down here where I can talk to you without straining my voice," he replied.

[*61*]

"Wait until I get another bite," replied Prickly Porky, stripping off a long piece of bark. Then with this to chew on, he came halfway down the tree and made himself comfortable on a big limb. "Now, what is it you've got on your mind?" he demanded.

At once Jimmy told him the queer story Peter Rabbit had told. "I've been sent up here to find out if you have seen this legless, headless, tailless creature. Have you?" he concluded.

Prickly Porky slowly shook his head. "No," said he. "I've been right here all the time, and I

[62]

haven't seen any such creature."

"That's all I want to know," replied Jimmy. "Peter Rabbit's got something the matter with his eyes, and I'm going straight back to the Old Briar-patch to tell him so. Much obliged." With that Jimmy started back the way he had come, grumbling to himself.

VIII

Prickly Porky Nearly Chokes

HARDLY was Jimmy Skunk be-
yond sight and hearing,
after having made his call, than
Redeye the Vireo, whose home is
in a tree just at the foot of the
hill where Prickly Porky lives,
heard a very strange noise. He
was very busy, was Redeye, telling
all who would listen how happy
he was and what a beautiful

[*64*]

world this is. Redeye seems to think that this is his special mission in life, that he was put in the Green Forest for this one special purpose—to sing all day long, even in the hottest weather when other birds forget to sing, his little song of gladness and happiness. It never seems to enter his head that he is making other people happy just by being happy himself and saying so.

At first he hardly noticed the strange noise, but when he stopped singing for a bit of a rest, he heard it very plainly, and it sounded so very queer that he

[65]

flew up the hill toward the place from which it seemed to come, and there his bright eyes soon discovered Prickly Porky. Right away he saw that Prickly Porky was in some kind of trouble, and that it was he who was making the queer noise. Prickly Porky was on the ground at the foot of a tree, and he was rolling over and kicking and clawing at his mouth, from which a little piece of bark was hanging. It was such a strange performance that Red-eye simply stared for a minute. Then in a flash it came to him what it meant. Prickly Porky was

[66]

choking, and if something wasn't done to help him, he might choke to death!

Now there was nothing that Redeye himself could do to help, for he was too small. He must get help somewhere else, and he must do it quickly. Anxiously he looked this way and that way, but there was no one in sight. Then he remembered that Unc' Billy Possum's hollow tree was not far away. Perhaps Unc' Billy could help. He hoped that Unc' Billy was at home, and he wasted no time in finding out. Unc' Billy was at home, and when he heard

[67]

that his old friend Prickly Porky was in trouble, he hurried up the hill as fast as ever he could. He saw right away what was the trouble.

"Yo' keep still just a minute, Brer Porky!" he commanded, for he did not dare go very near while Prickly Porky was rolling and kicking around so, for fear that he would get against some of the thousand little spears Prickly Porky carries hidden in his coat. Prickly Porky did as he was told. Indeed, he was so weak from his long struggle that he was glad to. Unc' Billy caught hold of the

[*68*]

Unc' Billy caught hold of the piece of bark
hanging from Prickly Porky's mouth

piece of bark hanging from Prickly Porky's mouth. Then he braced himself and pulled with all his might. For a minute the piece of bark held. Then it gave way so suddenly that Unc' Billy fell over flat on his back. Unc' Billy scrambled to his feet and looked reprovingly at Prickly Porky, who lay panting for breath, and with big tears rolling down his face.

"Ah cert'nly am surprised, Brer Porky; Ah cert'nly am surprised that yo' should be so greedy that yo' choke yo'self," said Unc' Billy, shaking his head.

Prickly Porky grinned weakly and rather foolishly. "It wasn't greed, Unc' Billy. It wasn't greed at all," he replied.

"Then what was it, may Ah ask?" demanded Unc' Billy severely.

"I thought of something funny right in the middle of my meal, and I laughed just as I started to swallow, and the piece of bark went down the wrong way," explained Prickly Porky. And then, as if the mere thought of the thing that had made him laugh before was too much for him, he began to laugh again. He laughed

[71]

and laughed and laughed, until finally Unc' Billy quite lost patience.

"Yo' cert'nly have lost your manners, Brer Porky!" he snapped.

Prickly Porky wiped the tears from his eyes. "Come closer so that I can whisper, Unc' Billy," said he.

A little bit suspiciously Unc' Billy came near enough for Prickly Porky to whisper, and when he had finished, Unc' Billy was wiping tears of laughter from his own eyes.

IX

Jimmy Skunk and Unc' Billy Possum Tell Different Stories

THE little people of the Green Meadows and the Green Forest didn't know what to believe. First came Peter Rabbit with the strangest kind of a story about being chased by a terrible creature without legs, head, or tail. He said that it had come down the hill where Prickly

Porky the Porcupine lives in the Green Forest. Jimmy Skunk had been sent to call on Prickly Porky and ask him if he had seen any strange creature such as Peter Rabbit had told about. Prickly Porky had said that he hadn't seen any stranger in that part of the Green Forest, and Jimmy had straightway returned to the Green Meadows and told all his friends there that Peter Rabbit must have had something the matter with his eyes or else was crazy, for Prickly Porky hadn't been away from home and yet had seen nothing unusual.

At the same time, Unc' Billy

Possum was going about in the Green Forest telling everybody whom he met that he had called on Prickly Porky, and that Prickly Porky had told him that Peter Rabbit undoubtedly had seen something strange. Of course, Jimmy Skunk's story soon spread through the Green Forest, and Unc' Billy Possum's story soon spread over the Green Meadows, and so nobody knew what to believe or think. If Jimmy Skunk was right, why, Peter Rabbit's queer story wasn't to be believed at all. If Unc' Billy was right, why, Peter's story wasn't as crazy as it sounded.

Of course, all this aroused a great deal of talk and curiosity, and those who had the most courage began to make visits to the hill where Prickly Porky lives to see if they could see for themselves anything out of the ordinary. But they always found that part of the Green Forest just as usual and always, if they saw Prickly Porky at all, he seemed to be fast asleep, and no one liked to wake him to ask questions. Little by little they began to think that Jimmy Skunk was right, and that Peter Rabbit's terrible creature existed only in Peter's imagination.

About this time Unc' Billy told of having just such an experience as Peter had. It happened exactly as it did with Peter, very early in the morning, when he was passing the foot of the hill where Prickly Porky lives.

"Ah was just passing along, minding mah own business, when Ah heard a noise up on the hill behind me," said Unc' Billy, "and when Ah looked up, there was something coming straight down at me, and Ah couldn't see any legs or head or tail."

"What did you do, Unc' Billy?" asked Bobby Coon.

"What did Ah do? Ah did just

*Unc' Billy told of having just such an experience
as Peter had*

what yo'alls would have done—
Ah done run!" replied Unc' Billy,
looking around the little circle of
forest and meadow people, listening with round eyes and open
mouths. "Yes, Sah, Ah done run,
and Ah didn't turn around until
Ah was safe in mah holler tree."

"Pooh!" sneered Reddy Fox,
who had been listening. "You're
a coward. I wouldn't have run! I
would have waited and found out
what it was. You and Peter Rabbit would run away from your
own shadows."

"You don't dare go there yourself at daybreak tomorrow!" re-
torted Unc' Billy.

"I do too!" declared Reddy angrily, though he didn't have the least intention of going.

"All right. Ah'm going to be in a tree where Ah can watch tomorrow mo'ning and see if yo' are as brave as yo' talk," declared Unc' Billy.

Then Reddy knew that he would have to go or else be called a coward. "I'll be there," he snarled angrily, as he slunk away.

X

Unc' Billy Possum Tells Jimmy Skunk a Secret

Be sure before you drop a friend
That you've done nothing to offend.

A FRIEND is always worth keeping. Unc' Billy Possum says
so, and he knows. He ought
to, for he has made a lot of
them in the Green Forest and on

the Green Meadows, in spite of the pranks he has cut up and the tricks he has played. And when Unc' Billy makes a friend, he keeps him. He says that it is easier and a lot better to keep a friend than to make a new one. And this is the way he goes about it: Whenever he finds that a friend is angry with him, he refuses to be angry himself. Instead, he goes to that friend, finds out what the trouble is, explains it all away, and then does something nice.

Jimmy Skunk and Unc' Billy had been friends from the time that Unc' Billy came up from ol'

[*82*]

Virginny to live in the Green Forest. In fact, they had been partners in stealing eggs from the henhouse of Farmer Brown's boy. So when Jimmy Skunk, who had made a special call on Prickly Porky to find out if he had seen the strange creature without head, tail, or legs, told everybody that Prickly Porky had seen nothing of such a creature, he was very much put out and quite offended to hear that Unc' Billy was telling how Prickly Porky had said that Peter might really have some reason for his queer story. It seemed to him that either Prickly

Porky had told an untruth or that Unc' Billy was telling an untruth. It made him very angry.

The afternoon of the day when Unc' Billy had dared Reddy Fox to go at sunup the next morning to the hill where Prickly Porky lives, he met Jimmy Skunk coming down the Crooked Little Path. Jimmy scowled and was going to pass without so much as speaking. Unc' Billy's shrewd little eyes twinkled, and he grinned as only Unc' Billy can grin. "Howdy, Brer Skunk," said he.

Jimmy just frowned harder than ever and tried to pass.

"Howdy, Brer Skunk," repeated

HARRISON CADY

*He met Jimmy Skunk coming down
the Crooked Little Path*

Unc' Billy Possum. "Yo' must have something on your mind."

Jimmy Skunk stopped. "I have!" he snapped. "I want to know whether it is you or Prickly Porky who has been telling an untruth. He told me that he hadn't seen anything like what Peter Rabbit said chased him, and you've been telling around how he told you that Peter may have had good grounds for that foolish story. If Peter saw that thing, Prickly Porky would know it, for he hasn't been away from home this summer. Why would he tell me that he hasn't seen it if he has?"

"Don' be hasty, Brer Skunk. Don' be hasty," replied Unc' Billy soothingly. "Ah haven't said that Brer Porky told me that he had seen the thing that Peter says chased him. He told the truth when he told you that he hadn't seen any stranger around his hill. What he told me was that—" Here Unc' Billy whispered.

Jimmy Skunk's face cleared. "That's different," said he.

"Of course it is," replied Unc' Billy. "Yo' see, Peter did see something strange, even if Brer Porky didn't. Ah have seen it mahself, and now Ah invites yo' to be over at the foot of Brer Porky's

[87]

hill at sunup tomorrow mo'ning and see what happens when Brer Fox tries to show how brave he is. Only don' forget that it's a secret."

Jimmy was chuckling by this time. "I won't forget, and I'll be there," he promised. "I'm glad to know that nobody has been telling untruths, and I beg your pardon, Unc' Billy, for thinking you might have been."

"Don' mention it, Brer Skunk, don' mention it. Ah'll be looking fo' yo' tomorrow mo'ning," replied Unc' Billy, with a sly wink that made Jimmy laugh aloud.

XI

What Happened
to Reddy Fox

REDDY FOX wished with all his
might that he had kept his
tongue still about not being
afraid to meet the strange creature that had given Peter Rabbit
such a fright. When he had
boasted that he would stop and
find out all about it if he happened to meet it, he didn't have
the least intention of doing any-

thing of the kind. He was just idly boasting and nothing more. You see, Reddy is one of the greatest boasters in the Green Forest or on the Green Meadows. He likes to strut around and talk big. But like most boasters, he is a coward at heart.

Unc' Billy Possum knew this, and that is why he dared Reddy to go the next morning to the foot of the hill where Prickly Porky the Porcupine lives, and where Peter Rabbit had had his strange adventure, and where Unc' Billy himself claimed to have seen the same strange crea-

[*90*]

ture without head, tail, or legs which had so frightened Peter. Unc' Billy had said that he would be there himself up in a tree where he could see whether Reddy really did come or not, and so there was nothing for Reddy to do but to go and make good his foolish boast, if the strange creature should appear. You see, a number of little people had heard him boast and had heard Unc' Billy dare him, and he knew that if he didn't make good, he would never hear the end of it and would be called a coward by everybody.

Reddy didn't sleep at all well that afternoon, and when at dusk he started to hunt for his supper, he found that he had lost his appetite. Instead of hunting, he spent most of the night in trying to think of some good reason for not appearing at Prickly Porky's hill at daybreak. But think as he would, he couldn't think of a single excuse that would sound reasonable. "If only Bowser the Hound wasn't chained up at night, I would get him to chase me, and then I would have the very best kind of an excuse," thought he. But he knew that

Bowser was chained. Nevertheless he did go up to Farmer Brown's dooryard to make sure. It was just as he expected—Bowser was chained.

Reddy sneaked away without even a look at Farmer Brown's henhouse. He didn't see that the door had carelessly been left open, and even if he had, it would have made no difference. He hadn't a bit of appetite. No, Sir. Reddy Fox wouldn't have eaten the fattest chicken there if it had been right before him. All he could think of was that queer story told by Peter Rabbit and

HARRISON CADY

*He just wandered about restlessly, waiting
for daybreak*

Unc' Billy Possum, and the scrape
he had got himself into by his
foolish boasting. He just wandered about restlessly, waiting for
daybreak and hoping that something would turn up to prevent
him from going to Prickly Porky's
hill. He didn't dare to tell old
Granny Fox about it. He knew
just what she would say. It
seemed as if he could hear her
sharp voice and the very words:

"Serves you right for boasting
about something you don't know
anything about. How many times
have I told you that no good
comes of boasting? A wise Fox

never goes near strange things until he has found out all about them. That is the only way to keep out of trouble and live to a ripe old age. Wisdom is nothing but knowledge, and a wise Fox always knows what he is doing."

So Reddy wandered about all the long night. It seemed as if it never would pass, and yet he wished it would last forever. The more he thought about it, the more afraid he grew. At last he saw the first beams from jolly, round, red Mr. Sun creeping through the Green Forest. The

[*96*]

time had come, and he must choose between making his boast good or being called a coward by everybody. Very, very slowly, Reddy Fox began to walk toward the hill where Prickly Porky lives.

XII

What Reddy Fox Saw and Did

Who guards his tongue as he would keep
  A treasure rich and rare,
Will keep himself from trouble free,
  And dodge both fear and care.

THE trouble with a great many people is that they remember this too late. Reddy Fox is one of these. Reddy is smart and sly and clever in some ways, but he hasn't learned yet to guard his tongue, and half the trouble he gets into is because of that unruly member. You see, it is a boastful tongue and an untruthful tongue, and that is the worst combination for making trouble that I know of. It has landed him in all kinds of scrapes in the past, and here he was in another, all on account of that tongue.

Jolly, round, red Mr. Sun had kicked his rosy blankets off and was smiling down on the Great World as he began his daily climb up in the blue, blue sky. The Jolly Little Sunbeams were already dancing through the

[*99*]

Green Forest, chasing out the Black Shadows, and Reddy knew that it was high time for him to be over by the hill where Prickly Porky the Porcupine lives. With lagging steps he sneaked along from tree to tree, peering out from behind each anxiously, afraid to go on, and still more afraid not to, for fear that he would be called a coward.

He had almost reached the foot of the hill without seeing any-thing out of the usual and with-out any signs of Unc' Billy Pos-sum. He was just beginning to hope that Unc' Billy wasn't there, as he had said he would be, when a voice right over his head said:

"Ah cert'nly am glad to see that yo' are as good as your word, Brer Fox, fo' we need someone brave like yo' to find out what this strange creature is that has been chasing we-uns."

Reddy looked up with a sickly grin. There sat Unc' Billy Possum in a pine tree right over his head. He knew now that there was no backing out; he had got to go on. He tried to swagger and look very bold and brave.

"I told you I'm not afraid. If there's anything queer around

here, I'll find out what it is,"
he once more boasted, but Unc'
Billy noticed that his voice
sounded just a wee bit trembly.

"Keep right on to the foot of
the hill; that's where Ah saw it
yesterday. My, Ah'm glad that
we've got someone so truly
brave!" replied Unc' Billy.

Reddy looked at him sharply,
but there wasn't a trace of a
smile on Unc' Billy's face, and
Reddy couldn't tell whether Unc'
Billy was making fun of him or
not. So, there being nothing else
to do, he went on. He reached
the foot of the hill without see-

[*102*]

ing or hearing a thing out of the usual. The Green Forest seemed just as it always had seemed. Red-eye the Vireo was pouring out his little song of gladness, quite as if everything was just as it should be. Reddy's courage began to come back. Nothing had happened, and nothing was going to happen. Of course not! It was all some of Peter Rabbit's foolishness. Someday he would catch Peter Rabbit and put an end to such silly tales.

"Ah! What was that?" Reddy's sharp ears had caught a sound up near the top of the hill. He stopped short and looked up. For just a little wee minute Reddy couldn't believe that his eyes saw right. Coming down the hill straight toward him was the strangest thing he ever had seen. He couldn't see any legs. He couldn't see any head. He couldn't see any tail. It was round like a ball, but it was the strangest-looking ball that ever was. It was covered with old leaves. Reddy wouldn't have believed that it was alive but for the noises it was making. For just a wee minute he stared, and then, what do you think he did? Why, he gave

Why, he gave a frightened yelp, and ran just as fast as he could make his legs go

a frightened yelp, put his tail between his legs, and ran just as
fast as he could make his legs go.
Yes, Sir, that's just what Reddy
Fox did.

XIII

Reddy Fox Is Very Miserable

WHEN Reddy Fox put his tail between his legs and started away from that terrible creature coming down the hill where Prickly Porky lives, he thought of nothing but of getting as far away as he could in the shortest time that he could, and so, with a little frightened yelp with every jump, he ran as he seldom had run before. He forgot all about Unc' Billy Possum watching from the safety of a big pine tree. He didn't see Jimmy Skunk poking his head out from behind an old stump and laughing fit to kill himself. When he reached the edge of the Green Forest, he didn't even see Peter Rabbit jump out of his path and dodge into a hollow log.

When Reddy was safely past, Peter came out. He sat up very straight, with his ears pointing right up to the sky and his eyes wide open with surprise as he stared after Reddy. "Why! Why, my gracious, I do believe Reddy has had a fright!" exclaimed Peter. Then, being Peter, he right away began to wonder what could have frightened Reddy so, and in a minute he thought of the strange creature which had frightened him a few days before. "I do believe that was it!" he cried. "I do believe it was. Reddy is coming from the direction of Prickly Porky's, and that was where I got my fright. I—I—"

Peter hesitated. The truth is he was wondering if he dared go up there and see if that strange creature without head, tail, or legs really was around again. He knew it would be a foolish thing to do, for he might walk right into danger. He knew that little Mrs. Peter was waiting for him over in the dear Old Briar-patch and that she would worry, for he ought to be there this very blessed minute. But he was very curious to know what had frightened Reddy so, and his curiosity, which has led him into so many scrapes, grew greater with every passing minute.

"It won't do any harm to go part way up there," thought Peter. "Perhaps I will find out

[*110*]

something without going way up there."

So, instead of starting for home as he should have done, he turned back through the Green Forest and, stopping every few hops to look and listen, made his way clear to the foot of the hill where Prickly Porky lives. There he hid under a little hemlock tree and looked in every direction for the strange creature which had frightened him so the last time he was there. But nobody was to be seen but Prickly Porky, Jimmy Skunk, and Unc' Billy Possum rolling around in the leaves at the top

[*111*]

of the hill and laughing fit to kill themselves.

"There's no danger here; that is sure," thought Peter shrewdly, "and I believe those fellows have been up to some trick."

With that he boldly hopped up the hill and joined them. "What's the joke?" he demanded.

"Did you meet Reddy Fox?" asked Jimmy Skunk, wiping the tears of laughter from his eyes.

"Did I meet him? Why, he almost ran into me and didn't see me at all. I guess he's running yet. Now, what's the joke?" Peter demanded.

[*112*]

When the others could stop laughing long enough, they gathered around Peter and told him something that sent Peter off into such a fit of laughter that it made his sides ache. "That's a good one on Reddy, and it was just as good a one on me," he declared. "Now who else can we scare?"

All of which shows that there was something very like mischief being planned on the hill where Prickly Porky the Porcupine lives.

XIV

Reddy Fox Tries To Keep Out of Sight

NEVER in all his life was Reddy Fox more uncomfortable in his mind. He knew that by this time everybody in the Green Forest, on the Green Meadows, around the Smiling Pool, and along the Laughing Brook, knew how he had put his tail between his legs and run with all his might at the first glimpse

[*114*]

of the strange creature which had rolled down the hill of Prickly Porky. And he was right; everybody did know it, and everybody was laughing about it. Unc' Billy Possum, Jimmy Skunk, Prickly Porky, and Peter Rabbit had seen him run, and you may be sure they told everybody they met about it, and news like that travels very fast.

It wouldn't have been so bad if he hadn't boasted beforehand that if he met the strange creature he would wait for it and find out what it was. As it was, he had run just as Peter Rabbit had run when

[*115*]

he saw it, and he had been just as much frightened as Peter had. Now, as he sneaked along trying to find something to eat, for he was hungry, he did his very best to keep out of sight. Usually he is very proud of his handsome red coat but now he wished that he could get rid of it. It is very hard to keep out of sight when you have bright-colored clothes. Presently Sammy Jay's sharp eyes spied him as he tried to crawl up on the young family of Mrs. Grouse. At once Sammy flew over there screaming at the top of his lungs:

[*116*]

"Reddy Fox is very brave when there's
no danger near;
But where there is, alas, alack! he
runs away in fear."

Reddy looked up at Sammy and snarled. It was of no use at all now to try to surprise and catch any of the family of Mrs. Grouse, so he turned around and hurried away, trying to escape from Sammy's sharp eyes. He had gone only a little way when a sharp voice called: "Coward! Coward! Coward!" It was Chatterer the Red Squirrel.

No sooner had he got out of

[*117*]

Chatterer's sight than he heard another voice. It was saying over and over:

"Dee, dee, dee! Oh, me, me!
Some folks can talk so very brave
And then such cowards be."

It was Tommy Tit the Chicka-dee. Reddy couldn't think of a thing to say in reply and so he hurried on, trying to find a place where he could be left in peace. But nowhere that he could go was he free from those taunting voices. Not even when he had crawled into his house was he free from them, for buzzing around his doorway was Bumble Bee, and Bumble was humming:

"Bumble, grumble, rumble, hum!
Reddy surely can run some."

Late that afternoon old Granny Fox called him out, and it was clear to see that Granny was very much put out about something. "What is this I hear everywhere I go about you being a coward?" she demanded, as soon as he put his head out of the doorway.

Reddy hung his head, and in a very shamefaced way he told her about the terrible fright he had had and all about the strange

[*119*]

creature without legs, head, or tail that had rolled down the hill.

"Serves you right for boasting!" snapped Granny. "How many times have I told you that no good comes of boasting? Probably somebody has played a trick on you. I've lived a good many years, and I never before heard of such a creature. If there were one, I'd have seen it before now. You go back into the house and stay there. You are a disgrace to the Fox family. I am going to have a look about and find out what is going on. If this is some trick, they'll find that old Granny Fox isn't so easily fooled."

[*120*]

XV

Old Granny Fox Investigates

IN-VEST-I-GATE is a great big word, but its meaning is very simple. To in-vest-i-gate is to look into and try to find out all about something. That is what old Granny Fox started to do after Reddy had told her about the terrible fright he had had at the hill where Prickly Porky lives.

Now old Granny Fox is very sly

[*121*]

and smart and clever, as you all know. Compared with her, Reddy Fox is almost stupid. He may be as sly and smart and clever some day, but he has got a lot to learn before then. Now if it had been Reddy who was going to investigate, he would have gone straight over to Prickly Porky's hill and looked around and asked sly questions, and everybody whom he met would have known that he was trying to find out something.

But old Granny Fox did nothing of the kind. Oh, my, no! She went about hunting her dinner just as usual and didn't appear

[*122*]

to be paying the least attention to what was going on about her. With her nose to the ground she ran this way and ran that way as if hunting for a trail. She peered into old hollow logs and looked under little brush piles, and so, in course of time, she came to the hill where Prickly Porky lives.

Now Reddy had told Granny that the terrible creature that had so frightened him had rolled down the hill at him, for he was at the bottom. Granny had heard that the same thing had happened to Peter Rabbit and to Unc' Billy Possum. So instead of coming to the hill along the hollow at the bottom, she came to it from the other way. "If there is anything there, I'll be behind it instead of in front of it," she thought shrewdly.

As she drew near where Prickly Porky lives, she kept eyes and ears wide open, all the time pretending to pay attention to nothing but the hunt for her dinner. No one would ever have guessed that she was thinking of anything else. She ran this way and that way all over the hill, but nothing out of the usual did she see or hear excepting one thing: she did find some queer marks down the hill

As she drew near where Prickly Porky lives,
she kept eyes and ears wide open

as if something might have rolled there. She followed these down to the bottom, but there they disappeared.

As she was trotting home along the Lone Little Path through the Green Forest, she met Unc' Billy Possum. No, she didn't exactly meet him, because he saw her before she saw him, and he promptly climbed a tree.

"Ah suppose yo'all heard of the terrible creature that scared Reddy almost out of his wits early this mo'ning," said Unc' Billy.

Granny stopped and looked up. "It doesn't take much to scare the young and innocent, Mr. Possum," she replied. "I don't believe all I hear. I've just been hunting all over the hill where Prickly Porky lives, and I couldn't find so much as a Wood Mouse for dinner. Do you believe such a foolish tale, Mr. Possum?"

Unc' Billy coughed behind one hand. "Yes, Mrs. Fox, Ah confess Ah done have to believe it," he replied. "Yo' see, Ah done see that thing mah own self, and Ah just naturally has to believe mah own eyes."

"Huh! I'd like to see it! Maybe I'd believe it then!" snapped Granny Fox.

"The only time to see it is just at sunup," replied Unc' Billy. "Anybody that comes along through that hollow at the foot of Brer Porky's hill at sunup is likely never to forget it. Ah wouldn't do it again. No, Sah, once is enough fo' your Unc' Billy."

"Huh!" snorted Granny and trotted on.

Unc' Billy watched her out of sight and grinned broadly. "As sho' as Brer Sun gets up tomorrow mo'ning, ol' Granny Fox will be there," he chuckled. "Ah must get word to Brer Porky and Brer Skunk and Brer Rabbit."

XVI

Old Granny Fox
Loses Her Dignity

UNC' BILLY POSSUM had passed
the word along to Jimmy
Skunk, Peter Rabbit, and Prickly
Porky that old Granny Fox would
be on hand at sunup to see
for herself the strange creature
which had frightened Reddy
Fox at the foot of the hill where
Prickly Porky lives. How did Unc'
Billy know? Well, he just guessed.

[*129*]

He is quite as shrewd and clever as Granny Fox herself, and when he told her that the only time the strange creature everybody was talking about was seen was at sunup, he guessed by the very way she sniffed and pretended not to believe it all that she would visit Prickly Porky's hill the next morning.

"The ol' lady suspects that there is some trick, and we-uns have got to be very careful," warned Unc' Billy, as he and his three friends put their heads together in the early evening. "She is done bound to come snooping around

[130]

before sunup," he continued, "and we-uns must be out of sight, all excepting Brer Porky. She'll come just the way she did this afternoon—from back of the hill instead of along the holler."

Unc' Billy was quite right. Old Granny Fox felt very sure that someone was playing tricks, so she didn't wait until jolly, round, red Mr. Sun was out of bed. She was at the top of the hill where Prickly Porky lives a full hour before sunup, and there she sat down to wait. She couldn't see or hear anything in the least suspicious. You see, Unc' Billy Possum

[*131*]

was quite out of sight, as he sat in the thickest part of a hemlock tree, and Peter Rabbit was sitting perfectly still in a hollow log, and Jimmy Skunk wasn't showing so much as the tip of his nose, as he lay just inside the doorway of an old house under the roots of a big stump. Only Prickly Porky was to be seen, and he seemed to be asleep in his favorite tree. Everything seemed to be just as old Granny Fox had seen it a hundred times before.

At last the Jolly Little Sunbeams began to dance through the Green Forest, chasing out the

Black Shadows. Redeye the Vireo awoke and at once began to sing, as is his way, not even waiting to get a mouthful of breakfast. Prickly Porky yawned and grunted. Then he climbed down from the tree he had been sitting in, walked slowly over to another, started to climb it, changed his mind, and began to poke around in the dead leaves. Old Granny Fox arose and slowly stretched. She glanced at Prickly Porky contemptuously. She had seen him act in this stupid, uncertain way dozens of times before. Then slowly, watching out sharply on both sides of her, with-

[*133*]

out appearing to do so, she walked down the hill to the hollow at the foot.

Now old Granny Fox can be very dignified when she wants to be, and she was now. She didn't hurry the least little bit. She carried her big, plumy tail just so. And she didn't once look behind her, for she felt sure that there was nothing out of the way there, and to have done so would have been quite undignified. She had reached the bottom of the hill and was walking along the hollow, smiling to herself to think how easily some people are fright-

[*134*]

ened, when her sharp ears caught a sound on the hill behind her. She turned like a flash and then—well, for a minute old Granny Fox was too surprised to do anything but stare. There, rolling down the hill straight towards her, was the very thing Reddy had told her about.

At first Granny decided to stay right where she was and find out what this thing was, but the nearer it got, the stranger and more terrible it seemed. It was just a great ball all covered with dried leaves, and yet somehow Granny felt sure that it was alive, although she could see no head or tail or legs.

[*135*]

The nearer it got, the stranger and more terrible it seemed. Then Granny forgot her dignity. Yes, Sir, she forgot her dignity. In fact, she quite lost it altogether. Granny Fox ran just as Reddy had run!

XVII

Granny Fox Catches Peter Rabbit

Now listen to this little tale
  That deals somewhat with folly,
And shows how sometimes one may be
  A little bit too jolly.

NO SOONER was old Granny Fox out of sight, running as if she thought that every jump might be her last, than Jimmy Skunk came out from the hole under a big stump where he had been hiding, Peter Rabbit came out of the hollow log from which he had been peeping, and Unc' Billy Possum dropped down from the hemlock tree in which he had so carefully kept out of sight, and all three began to dance around Prickly Porky, laughing as if they were trying to split their sides.

"Ho, ho, ho!" shouted Jimmy Skunk. "I wonder what Reddy Fox would have said if he could have seen old Granny go down that hollow!"

"Ha, ha, ha!" shouted Peter Rabbit. "Did you see how her eyes popped out?"

[138]

"Hee, hee, hee!" squeaked Unc' Billy Possum in his funny, cracked voice. "Ah reckons she am bound to have sore feet if she keeps on running the way she started."

Prickly Porky didn't say a word. He just smiled in a quiet sort of way, as he slowly climbed up to the top of the hill.

Now old Granny Fox had been badly frightened. Who wouldn't have been at seeing a strange creature without head, tail, or legs rolling downhill straight toward them? But Granny was too old and wise to run very far without cause. She was hardly out of sight

[139]

of the four little scamps who had been watching her, when she stopped to see if that strange creature were following her. It didn't take her long to decide that it wasn't. Then she did some quick thinking.

"I said beforehand that there was some trick, and now I'm sure of it," she muttered. "I have an idea that that good-for-nothing old Billy Possum knows something about it, and I'm just going back to find out."

She wasted no time thinking about it, but began to steal back the way she had come. Now no one is lighter of foot than old

[*140*]

Granny Fox, and no one knows better how to keep out of sight. From tree to tree she crawled, sometimes flat on her stomach, until at last she reached the foot of the hill where she had just had such a fright. There was nothing to be seen there, but up at the top of the hill she saw something that made a fierce, angry gleam come into her yellow eyes. Then she smiled grimly. "The last laugh always is the best laugh, and this time I guess it is going to be mine," she said to herself. Very slowly and carefully, so as not to so much as rustle a leaf, she began to crawl around so as

[*141*]

to come up on the back side of the hill.

Now what old Granny Fox had seen was Peter Rabbit and Jimmy Skunk and Unc' Billy Possum rolling over and over in the dried leaves, turning somersaults, and shouting and laughing, while Prickly Porky sat looking on and smiling. Granny knew well enough what was tickling them so, and she knew too that they didn't dream but that she was still running away in fright. At last they were so tired with their good time that they just had to stop for a rest.

"Oh dear, I'm all out of breath," panted Peter, as he threw himself flat on the ground. "That was the funniest thing I ever saw. I wonder who we—"

Peter didn't finish. No, Sir, Peter didn't finish. Instead, he gave a frightened shriek as something red flashed out from under a low-growing hemlock tree close behind him, and two black paws pinned him down, and sharp teeth caught him by the back of the neck. Old Granny Fox had caught Peter Rabbit at last!

XVIII

A Friend in Need
Is a Friend Indeed

The friendship which is truest, best,
Is that which meets the trouble test.

N<small>O ONE</small> really knows who his best friends are until he gets in trouble. When everything is lovely and there is no sign of trouble anywhere, one may have ever and ever so many friends. At least, it may seem so. But let trouble come, and all too often these seeming friends disappear as if by magic, until only a few, sometimes a very few, are left. These are the real friends, the true friends, and they are worth more than all the others put together. Remember that if you are a true friend to anyone, you will stand by him and help him, no matter what happens. Sometimes it is almost worth while getting into trouble just to find out who your real friends are.

Peter Rabbit found out who some of his truest friends are when, because of his own carelessness, old Granny Fox caught him.

Peter has been in many tight places and had many terrible frights in his life, but never did he feel quite so helpless and hopeless as when he felt the black paws of old Granny Fox pinning him down and Granny's sharp teeth in the loose skin on the back of his neck. All he could do was to kick with all his might, and kicking was quite useless, for Granny took great care to keep out of the way of those stout hind legs of his.

Many, many times Granny Fox had tried to catch Peter, and always before Peter had been too smart for her, and had just made

[*146*]

fun of her and laughed at her.
Now it was her turn to laugh, all
because he had been careless and
foolish. You see, Peter had been so
sure that Granny had had such a
fright when she ran away from the
strange creature that rolled down
Prickly Porky's hill at her, that
she wouldn't think of coming
back, and so he had just given
himself up to enjoying Granny's
fright. At Peter's screams of fright,
Unc' Billy Possum scampered for
the nearest tree, and Jimmy Skunk
dodged behind a big stump. You
see, it was so sudden that they
really didn't know what had happened. But Prickly Porky, whom

some people call stupid, made no move to run away. He happened to be looking at Peter when Granny caught him, and so he knew just what it meant. A spark of anger flashed in his usually dull eyes and for once in his life Prickly Porky moved quickly. The thousand little spears hidden in his coat suddenly stood on end and Prickly Porky made a fierce little rush forward.

"Drop him!" he grunted.

Granny Fox just snarled and backed away, dragging Peter with her and keeping him between Prickly Porky and herself.

*Granny Fox snarled and backed away, dragging
Peter with her*

By this time Jimmy Skunk had recovered himself. You know he is not afraid of anybody or anything. He sprang out from behind the stump, looking a wee bit shamefaced, and started for old Granny Fox. "You let Peter Rabbit go!" he commanded in a very threatening way. Now the reason Jimmy Skunk is afraid of nobody is because he carries with him a little bag of very strong perfume which makes everybody sick but himself. Granny Fox knows all about this. For just a minute she hesitated. Then she thought that if Jimmy used it, it would be as

[*150*]

bad for Peter as for her, and she didn't believe Jimmy would use it. So she kept on backing away, dragging Peter with her. Then Unc' Billy Possum took a hand, and his was the bravest deed of all, for he knew that Granny was more than a match for him in a fight. He slipped down from the tree where he had sought safety, crept around behind Granny, and bit her sharply on one heel. Granny let go of Peter to turn and snap at Unc' Billy. This was Peter's chance. He slipped out from under Granny's paws and in a flash was behind Prickly Porky

XIX

Jimmy Skunk Takes Word to Mrs. Peter

WHEN old Granny Fox found Prickly Porky, with his thousand little spears all pointing at her, standing between her and Peter Rabbit, she was the angriest old Fox ever seen. She didn't dare touch Prickly Porky, for she knew well enough what it would mean to get one of those sharp, barbed little spears in her skin. To think that she

[152]

actually had caught Peter Rabbit and then lost him was too provoking! It was more than her temper, never of the best, could stand. In her anger she dug up the leaves and earth with her feet, and all the time her tongue fairly flew as she called Prickly Porky, Jimmy Skunk, and Unc' Billy Possum everything bad she could think of. Her yellow eyes snapped so that it seemed almost as if sparks of fire flew from them. It made Peter shiver just to look at her.

Unc' Billy Possum, who, by slipping up behind her and biting one of her heels, had made

[153]

her let go of Peter, grinned down at her from a safe place in a tree. Jimmy Skunk stood grinning at her in the most provoking manner, and she couldn't do a thing about it, because she had no desire to have Jimmy use his little bag of perfume. So she talked herself out and then with many parting threats of what she would do, she started for home. Unc' Billy noticed that she limped a little with the foot he had nipped so hard, and he couldn't help feeling just a little bit sorry for her.

When she had gone, the others turned to Peter Rabbit to see how badly he had been hurt. They looked him all over and found that he wasn't much the worse for his rough experience. He was rather stiff and lame, and the back of his neck was very sore where Granny Fox had seized him, but he would be quite himself in a day or two.

"I must get home now," said he in a rather faint voice. "Mrs. Peter will be sure that something has happened to me and will be worried almost to death."

"No, you don't!" declared Jimmy Skunk. "You are going to stay right here where we can take care of you. It wouldn't be safe for you to try to go to the Old

Briar-patch now, because if you should meet Old Man Coyote or Reddy Fox or Whitetail the Marshhawk, you would not be able to run fast enough to get away. I will go down and tell Mrs. Peter, and you will make yourself comfortable in the old house behind that stump where I was hiding."

Peter tried to insist on going home, but the others wouldn't hear of it, and Jimmy Skunk settled the matter by starting for the dear Old Briar-patch. He found little Mrs. Peter anxiously looking toward the Green Forest for some sign of Peter.

[*156*]

"Oh!" she cried. "Do tell me quickly what has happened to Peter."

"Oh!" she cried, "you have come to bring me bad news. Do tell me quickly what has happened to Peter!"

"Nothing much has happened to Peter," replied Jimmy promptly. Then in the drollest way he told all about the fright of Granny Fox when she first saw the terrible creature rolling down the hill, and all that happened after, but he took great care to make light of Peter's escape, and explained that he was just going to rest up there on Prickly Porky's hill for that day and would be home the next night. But little Mrs. Peter wasn't wholly satisfied.

"I've begged him and begged him to keep away from the Green Forest," said she, "but now if he is hurt so that he can't come home, he needs me, and I'm going straight up there myself!"

Nothing that Jimmy could say had the least effect, and so at last he agreed to take her to Peter. And so, hopping behind Jimmy Skunk, timid little Mrs. Peter Rabbit actually went into the Green Forest of which she was so much afraid, which shows how brave love can be sometimes.

XX

A Plot To Frighten Old Man Coyote

Mischief leads to mischief, for it is
almost sure
To never, never be content without a
little more.

Now you would think that after Peter Rabbit's very, very narrow escape from the clutches of Old Granny Fox that Jimmy Skunk, Unc' Billy Possum, Peter Rabbit, and Prickly Porky

[*160*]

would have been satisfied with
the pranks they already had
played. No, Sir, they were not!
You see, when danger is over, it
is quickly forgotten. No sooner
had Peter been made comfortable
in the old house behind the big
stump on the hill where Prickly
Porky lives than the four scamps
began to wonder who else they
could scare with the terrible creature without head, legs, or tail
which had so frightened Reddy
and Old Granny Fox.

"There is Old Man Coyote;
he is forever frightening those
smaller and weaker than himself.

I'd just love to see him run,"
said Peter Rabbit.

"The very one!" cried Jimmy
Skunk. "I wonder if he would be
afraid. You know he is even
smarter than Granny Fox, and
though she was frightened at
first, she soon got over it. How
do you suppose we can get him
over here?"

"We-uns will take Brer Jay into
our secret. Brer Jay will tell Brer
Coyote that Brer Rabbit is up
here on Brer Porky's hill, hurt so
that he can't get home," said
Unc' Billy Possum. "That's all
Brer Jay need to say. Brer Coyote

[162]

is gwine to come up here hot foot with his tongue hanging out fo' that dinner he's sho' is waiting fo' him here."

"You won't do anything of the kind!" spoke up little Mrs. Peter, who, you know, had bravely left the dear Old Briar-patch and come up here in the Green Forest to take care of Peter. "Peter has had trouble enough already, and I'm not going to let him have any more, so there!"

"Peter isn't going to get into any trouble," spoke up Jimmy Skunk. "Peter and you are going to be just as safe as if you were

[*163*]

over in the Old Briar-patch, for
you will be in that old house
where nothing can harm you.
Now, please, Mrs. Peter, don't be
foolish. You don't like Old Man
Coyote, do you? You'd like to
see him get a great scare to make
up for the scares he has given
Peter and you, wouldn't you?"

Little Mrs. Peter was forced to
admit that she would, and after
a little more teasing she finally
agreed to let them try their plan
for giving Old Man Coyote a
scare. Sammy Jay happened along
just as Jimmy Skunk was starting
out to look for him, and when he

was told what was wanted of him, he agreed to do his part. You know Sammy is always ready for any mischief. Just as he started to look for Old Man Coyote, Unc' Billy Possum made another suggestion.

"We-uns have had a lot of fun with Reddy and Granny Fox," said he, "and now it seems to me that it is no more than fair to invite them over to see Old Man Coyote and what he will do when he first sees the terrible creature that has frightened them so. Granny knows now that there is nothing to be afraid of, and perhaps she will forget her anger if she has a chance to see Old Man Coyote run away. Yo' know she isn't wasting any love on him. What do yo' alls say?"

Peter and Mrs. Peter said "No!" right away, but Jimmy Skunk and Prickly Porky thought it a good idea, and, of course, Sammy Jay was willing. After a little, when it was once more pointed out to them how they would be perfectly safe in the old house behind the big stump, Peter and Mrs. Peter agreed, and Sammy started off on his errand.

XXI

Sammy Jay Delivers His Message

S AMMY JAY has been the bearer of so many messages that no one knows better than he how to deliver one. He knows when to be polite, and no one can be more polite than he. First he went over to the home of Reddy and Granny Fox and invited them to come over to the hill where Prickly Porky lives and see the terrible creature which had frightened them so give Old Man Coyote a scare. Both Reddy and Granny promptly said they would do nothing of the kind, that probably Sammy was engaged in some kind of mischief, and that, anyway, they knew that there was no such creature without head, legs, or tail, and though they had been fooled once, they didn't propose to be fooled again.

"All right," replied Sammy, quite as if it made no difference to him. "You admit that, smart as you are, you were fooled, and we thought you might like to see the

[*168*]

same thing happen to Old Man Coyote."

With this, he flew on his way to the Green Meadows to look for Old Man Coyote, and as he flew he chuckled to himself. "They'll be there," he muttered. "I know them well enough to know that nothing would keep them away when there is a chance to see someone else frightened, especially Old Man Coyote. They'll try to keep out of sight, but they'll be there."

Sammy found Old Man Coyote taking a sun bath. "Good morning, Mr. Coyote. I hope you are

[*169*]

*Sammy found Old Man Coyote taking
a sun bath*

feeling well," said Sammy in his politest manner.

"Fairly, fairly, thank you," replied Old Man Coyote, all the time watching Sammy sharply out of the corners of his shrewd eyes. "What's the news in the Green Forest?"

"There isn't any, that is, none to amount to anything," declared Sammy. "I never did see such a dull summer. Is there any news down here on the Green Meadows? I hear Danny Meadow Mouse has found his lost baby."

"So I hear," replied Old Man Coyote. "I tried to find it for

[*171*]

him. You know I believe in being neighborly."

Sammy grinned, for as he said this, Old Man Coyote had winked one eye ever so little, and Sammy knew very well that if he had found that lost baby, Danny Meadow Mouse would never have seen him again. "By the way," said Sammy in the most matter-of-fact tone, "as I was coming through the Green Forest, I saw Peter Rabbit over on the hill where Prickly Porky lives, and Peter seems to have been in some kind of trouble. He was so lame that he said he didn't dare try to go home to the Old Briar-patch

[*172*]

for fear that he might meet someone looking for a Rabbit dinner,
and he knew that, feeling as he
did, he wouldn't be able to save
himself. Peter is going to come
to a bad end someday if he
doesn't watch out."

"That depends on what you
call a bad end," replied Old Man
Coyote, with a sly grin. "It might
be bad for Peter and at the same
time be very good for someone
else."

Sammy laughed right out.
"That's one way of looking at
it," said he. "Well, I should hate
to have anything happen to Peter, because I have lots of fun

[*173*]

quarreling with him and should miss him dreadfully. I think I'll go up to the Old Orchard and see what is going on there."

Off flew Sammy in the direction of the Old Orchard, and once more he chuckled as he flew. He had seen Old Man Coyote's ears prick up ever so little when he had mentioned that Peter was over in the Green Forest so lame that he didn't dare go home. "Old Man Coyote will start for the Green Forest as soon as I am out of sight," thought Sammy. And that is just what Old Man Coyote did.

XXII

Old Man Coyote Loses His Appetite

HARDLY was Sammy Jay out of sight, flying toward the Old Orchard, before Old Man Coyote started for the Green Forest. He is very sharp, is Old Man Coyote, so sharp that it is not very often that he is fooled. If Sammy Jay had gone to him and told him what a splendid chance he would have to catch Peter

Rabbit if he hurried up to the Green Forest right away, Old Man Coyote would have suspected a trick of some kind. Sammy had been clever enough to know this. So he had just mentioned in the most matter-of-fact way that he had seen Peter over on Prickly Porky's hill and that Peter appeared to have been in trouble, so that he was too lame to go to his home in the dear Old Briarpatch. There wasn't even a hint that Old Man Coyote should go over there. This was what made him sure that the news about Peter was probably true.

[*176*]

Now as soon as Sammy was sure that Old Man Coyote couldn't see him, he headed straight for the Green Forest and the hill where Prickly Porky, Jimmy Skunk, Unc' Billy Possum, and Peter and Mrs. Peter Rabbit were waiting. As he flew, he saw Reddy Fox and old Granny Fox stretched flat behind an old log some distance away, but where they could see all that might happen.

"I knew they would be on hand," he chuckled.

When he reached the others, he reported that he had delivered the message to Old Man Coyote,

[*177*]

and that he was very sure, in fact, he was positive, that Old Man Coyote was already on his way there in the hope that he would be able to catch Peter Rabbit. It was decided that everybody but Peter should get out of sight at once. So Unc' Billy Possum climbed a tree. Jimmy Skunk crawled into a hollow log. Sammy Jay hid in the thickest part of a hemlock tree. Prickly Porky got behind a big stump right at the top of the hill. Little Mrs. Peter, with her heart going pit-a-pat, crept into the old house between the roots of this same old stump,

[*178*]

and only Peter was to be seen
when, at last, Old Man Coyote
came tiptoeing along the hollow
at the foot of the hill, as noiseless
as a gray shadow.

He saw Peter almost as soon as
Peter saw him, and the instant he
saw him, he stopped as still as if
he were made of stone. Peter took
a couple of steps, and it was very
plain to see that he was lame,
just as Sammy Jay had said.

"That good-for-nothing Jay told
the truth for once," thought Old
Man Coyote, with a hungry gleam
in his eyes.

Whenever Old Man Coyote

[*179*]

thought that Peter was not looking his way, he would crawl on
his stomach from one tree to another, always getting a little nearer
to Peter. He would lie perfectly
still when Peter seemed to be
looking toward him. Now, of
course, Peter knew just what was
going on, and he took the greatest care not to get more than a
couple of jumps away from the
old house under the big stump,
where Mrs. Peter was hiding and
wishing with all her might that
she and Peter were back in the
dear Old Briar-patch. It was very
still in the Green Forest save for
the song of happiness of Redeye

the Vireo who, if he knew what was going on, made no sign. My, but it was exciting to those who were watching!

Old Man Coyote had crept halfway up the hill, and Peter was wondering how much nearer he could let him get with safety, when a sudden grunting broke out right behind him. Peter knew what it meant and jumped to one side. Then down the hill, rolling straight toward Old Man Coyote, started the strange, headless, tail-less, legless creature that had so frightened Reddy and Granny Fox.

Old Man Coyote took one

good look, hesitated, looked again, and then turned tail and started for the Green Meadows as fast as his long legs would take him. It was plain to see that he was afraid, very much afraid. Quite suddenly he had lost his appetite.

XXIII

Buster Bear Gives
It All Away

I T WAS very clear that Old Man
Coyote wasn't thinking about
his stomach just then, but about
his legs and how fast they could
go. He had been halfway up
the hill when he first saw the
terrible creature without head,
tail, or legs rolling down straight
at him. He stopped only long
enough for one good look and
[183]

then he started for the bottom of the hill as fast as he could make his legs go. Now it is a very bad plan to run fast downhill. Yes, Sir, it is a very bad plan. You see, once you are started, it is not the easiest thing in the world to stop. And then again, you are quite likely to stub your toes.

This is what Old Man Coyote did. He stubbed his toes and turned a complete somersault. He looked so funny that the little scamps watching him had all they could do to keep from shouting right out. Old Granny Fox and Reddy Fox, looking on from a

[184]

safe distance, did laugh. You know they had not been friendly with Old Man Coyote since he came to live on the Green Meadows, and as they had themselves had a terrible fright when they first saw the strange creature, they rejoiced in seeing him frightened.

But Old Man Coyote didn't stop for a little thing like a tumble. Oh, my, no! He just rolled over on to his feet and was off again, harder than before. Now there are very few people who can see behind them without turning their heads, as Peter Rabbit can, and Old Man Coyote is

[185]

not one of them. Trying to watch behind him, he didn't see where he was going, and the first thing he knew he ran bump into—guess who! Why, Buster Bear, to be sure.

Where Buster had come from nobody knew, but there he was, as big as life. When Old Man Coyote ran into him, he growled a deep, provoked growl and whirled around with one big paw raised to cuff whoever had so nearly upset him. Old Man Coyote, more frightened than ever, yelped and ran harder than before, so that by the time Buster

Bear saw who it was who had run into him, he was safely out of reach and still running.

Then it was that Buster Bear first saw, rolling down the hill, the strange creature which had so frightened Old Man Coyote. Unc' Billy Possum, Jimmy Skunk, Sammy Jay, Peter Rabbit and Mrs. Peter, watching from safe hiding places, wondered if Buster would run too. If he did, it would be almost too good to be true. But he didn't. He looked first at the strange creature rolling down the hill, then at Old Man Coyote running as hard as ever

HARRISON CADY

*Buster Bear looked at the strange creature,
and his shrewd little eyes began to twinkle*

he could, and his shrewd little eyes began to twinkle. Then he began to laugh.

"Ha, ha, ha! Ho, ho, ho! Ha, ha, ho! I see you are up to your old tricks, Prickly Porky!" he shouted, as the strange creature rolled past, almost over his toes and brought up against a little tree at the foot of the hill.

Old Man Coyote heard him and stopped short and turned to see what it meant. Very slowly the strange creature unrolled and turned over. There was a head now, and a tail and four legs. It was none other than Prickly

Porky himself! There was no doubt about it, though he still looked very strange, for he was covered with dead leaves which clung to the thousand little spears hidden in his coat. Prickly Porky grinned.

"You shouldn't have given me away, Buster Bear, just because you have seen me roll downhill before, in the Great Woods where we both came from," said he.

"I think it was high time I did," replied Buster Bear, still chuckling. "You might have scared somebody to death down here where they don't know you."

[190]

Then everybody came out of their hiding places, laughing and talking all at once, as they told Buster Bear of the joke they had played on Old Man Coyote, and how it had all grown out of the fright Peter Rabbit had received when he just happened along as Prickly Porky was rolling downhill just for fun. As for Old Man Coyote, he sneaked away, grinding his teeth angrily. Like a great many other people, he couldn't take a joke on himself.

So Prickly Porky made himself at home in the Green Forest and took his place among the little people who live there. In just the

ADVENTURES OF PRICKLY PORKY

same way Old Man Coyote came
as a stranger to the Green Meadows and established himself there.
In the next book you may read
all about how he came to the
Green Meadows and of some of
his adventures there and in the
Green Forest.